THE TUB PEOPLE

BY **PAM CONRAD** ILLUSTRATIONS BY **RICHARD EGIELSKI**

A LAURA GERINGER BOOK
AN IMPRINT OF HARPERCOLLINSPUBLISHERS

The Tub People stood in a line all day on the edge of the bathtub. There were seven of them, and they always stood in the same order—the father, the mother, the grandmother, the doctor, the policeman, the child and the dog.

They were made out of wood, and their faces were very plain. They could smile or frown, or cry or laugh. Sometimes they would even wink at each other, but it hardly showed.

The father of the Tub People liked to play sea captain. He would take the mother, the grandmother and the child for a ride on the floating soap. The others stood on the edge of the tub and waved. Once in a while the child of the Tub People would slide off the soap into the warm bath.

"Help! Help!"

And the captain would rescue him.

"We're coming! We're coming!"

The policeman and the doctor liked to have water races, bobbing from one end of the tub to the other. The child would cheer. The grandmother would say, "Hush! You're very noisy."

When bathtime was over, the Tub People always lined up along the edge of the bathtub—the father, the mother, the grandmother, the doctor, the policeman, the child and the dog.

But one evening the bathwater began rushing down the drain before they were lined up, pulling all the Tub People this way and that. The soap danced over to the drain, turning and turning at the top of a whirlpool. Standing on the soap, getting dizzier and dizzier, was the child of the Tub People.

"Help! Help!"

But this time his father could not save him.

And the Tub Child disappeared down the drain without a sound.

The Tub Mother pressed her face to the grating. She looked and looked for her Tub Child. But she could not see him.

Later that night the Tub People lined up on the edge of the tub, just the six of them. The soap was soft and back in the soap dish. The washcloth made a lonely dripping sound as it hung from the faucet.

The Tub People felt very sad.

The next night the six Tub People climbed onto the washcloth raft. They called and called for their Tub Child. Of course, they knew exactly where their child had gone. But somehow they felt comforted by calling for him.

"Honey, where are you? Come home now. Please come back." But he did not answer.

Every evening the Tub People continued to float in the bathwater. But in time they stopped calling.

And they never winked at each other anymore.

Then an unusual thing happened. The bathwater began going down the drain slower and slower.

Big people came and peered into the tub. "What's the matter with the tub drain?" they asked. They filled the room with deep voices and blocked the light.

"What's the matter with the tub drain?"

The Tub People stood woodenly in their line. If they could have spoken, they would have shouted out what a terrible drain that was, and how it had sucked away their little Tub Child. But they were silent.

That afternoon, a big man came and pried off the drain cover, grunting as he worked. He shone a light down the drain and frowned. Then he pushed in a long wire and jiggled it up and down. Up and down.

"Come home now," the grandmother whispered.

And out of the drain popped the little Tub Child, wet and tired.

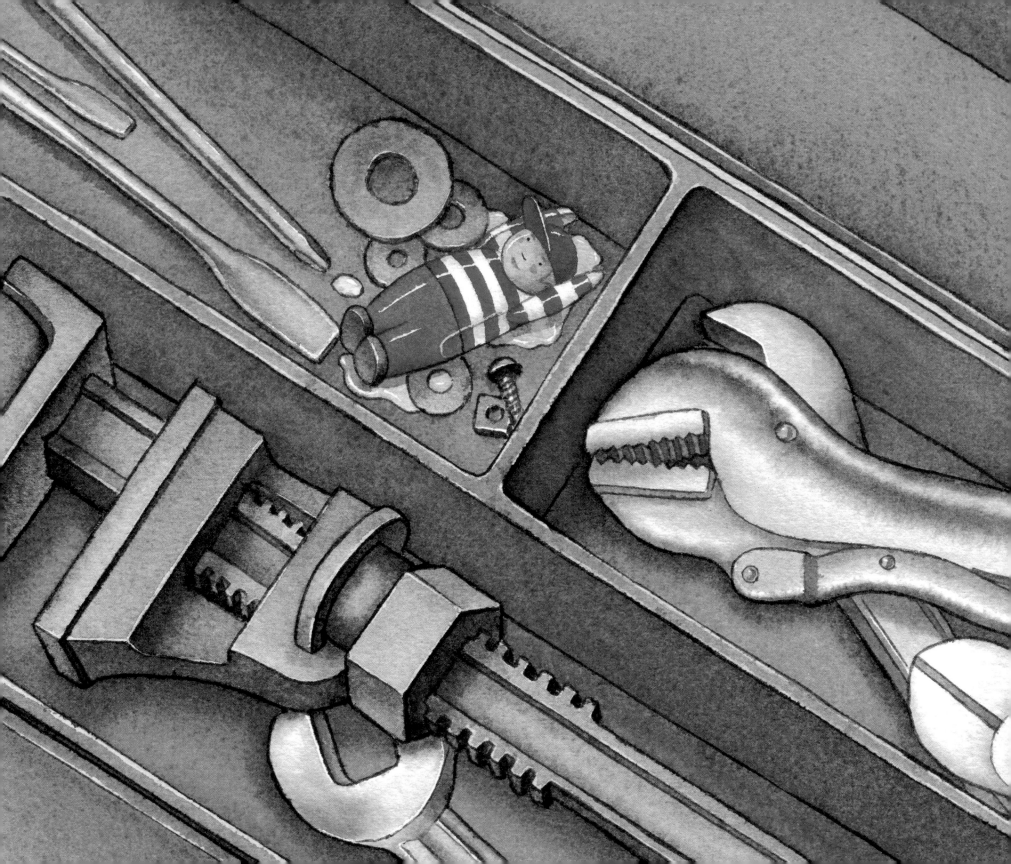

The Tub People stood in a line, quietly watching. One by one they smiled—the father, the mother, the grandmother, the doctor, the policeman and the dog. And the Tub Mother had little soapy tears running down her wooden cheeks.

But the big man did not look at them. He tossed the Tub Child into his toolbox, shut it with a click and left.

The Tub People waited for bathtime, hoping their Tub Child would come back.

But bathtime never came. It grew later and later, and still they waited, worrying all the while.

Finally, when they felt they could wait no longer, they were lifted up and carefully carried into a new room and gently placed on a large, soft bed! It seemed just like the water to them, except that it was dry and very firm.

And there were seven of them once again! The Tub Dog knocked his little wooden head against the Tub Child's head, and very quietly they all laughed.

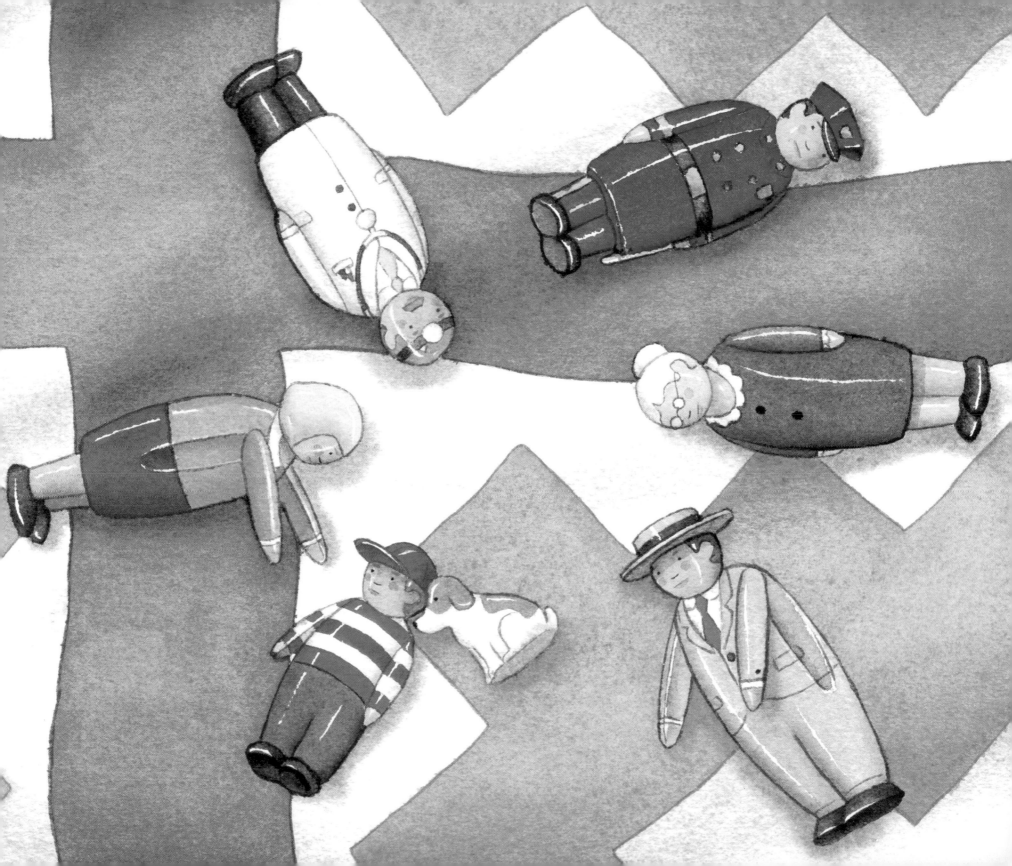

There was a thick quilt on the bed, and when it was all bunched up, they would go mountain climbing. The father liked to be the leader, and he would lead them up one side of the mountain, and then they would all tumble easily down the other.

The grandmother liked to hide under the pillow and have everyone come find her. The Tub Child liked to fall off the edge and have his father rescue him.

Each night when the lights went out, they lined up along the windowsill, just as they had along the bathtub edge—the father, the mother, the grandmother, the doctor, the policeman, the child and the dog.

But each morning, when the sun came shining in on them, something would be different. The Tub Child would be standing between the Tub Mother and the Tub Father, their sides barely touching.

And if you looked very, very closely, you would see they all had smiles on their small wooden faces.